ALICE IN BREXITLAND

ALICE IN
BREXITLAND

By Leavis Carroll

EBURY
PRESS

3 5 7 9 10 8 6 4

Ebury Press, an imprint of Ebury Publishing
20 Vauxhall Bridge Road
London SW1V 2SA

Ebury Press is part of the Penguin Random House group
of companies whose addresses can be found at
global.penguinrandomhouse.com

Penguin
Random House
UK

First published by Ebury Press in 2017

www.penguin.co.uk

A CIP catalogue record for this book is available
from the British Library

ISBN 9781785036965

Edited by Anna Mrowiec

Printed and bound in Great Britain by Clays Ltd, St Ives PLC

Penguin Random House is committed to a sustainable future
for our business, our readers and our planet. This book is
made from Forest Stewardship Council® certified paper.

To David Cameron, without whom
this book would not have been written.

Contents

These days, whene'er I watch the news
Or finger Twitter's app
Or else my Facebook feed peruse
With iPad on my lap
I cannot fail to darkly muse
'The world has gone to crap!'

No, rather it has gone insane
For every headline brings
More horrors no one can explain
More arrows and more slings
And how the news fills up your brain
With such unpleasant things!

Piers Morgan, Kim Jong-un, 4chan
Exploding phones, the *Mail*
Revenge porn, war against Iran
The zombie knife and kale
'Our long-term economic plan'
'Fake news', 'too big to fail'

And meanwhile one can always hear
The endless cyber-scream
Of commenters who live to jeer
And spread the latest meme

Think piece, hot take, white noise, fear,
'Screw you, 2016!'

But though the world is mad, all told
A balm has been supplied us
In Lewis Carroll's tale of old
Let his example guide us
For he turned madness into gold
Like some comedic Midas

And it is he (I'm sure you guessed)
This tale is modelled after
A barmy bard, whose writing blessed
The world with joy and laughter
And likewise I shall do my best
To leave it somewhat dafter

And so the reader I implore:
Come with me, hand in hand!
We'll swap our crazy country for
One madder and more grand
And as dear Alice did before
Fall into Wonderland…

Chapter I

Down the Brexit-hole

Alice sat by her sister on the riverbank and wondered if she might not die of boredom. This seemed to her a rather drab mode of death. 'Had I the choice,' thought Alice, 'I should prefer to be eaten by crocodile, or fall in a volcano.' These thoughts aside, it was clear she needed something to do. But what? She might have chased a butterfly, or plucked some daisies for a chain, but both of these things would require movement, and that was out of the question.

As a last resort, Alice glanced at the book her older sister was reading. Its cover bore these words: 'THE DEBATE SURROUNDING MEMBERSHIP OF THE EUROPEAN UNION'. She peeped inside, but saw in it no pictures or conversations. 'And what is the use of a book,' thought Alice, 'without pictures or conversations?' Moreover, she spotted among its strange, unwieldy words one that was all too familiar: 'Brexit'.

Alice shuddered, for all that she had heard from grown ups over the past few weeks was 'Brexit' this and 'referendum' that. When she had asked what a 'referendum' was (for it sounded like a magnificent beast with tusks and a woolly hide) she had been told it was an important decision and, like all decisions in the grown-up realm, it was to be made with reference to trade deals, deficits and something called 'GDP'.

Alice wished the world were not so stuffed with facts and figures – if only one could make decisions based on the first thing that popped into one's head! Imagine the laws we might have then: free scones for every family; a blanket ban on governesses; even help to buy one's dollhouse! Yes, she thought, that would surely be a fine state of affairs.

The day was hot and drowsy, so Alice decided to lie back, close her eyes and pursue this train of thought. She was lazily considering whether Dinah, her cat, should not be Home Secretary, when suddenly a white rabbit ran by. This would not have been *so* remarkable had the rabbit not been wearing a navy-blue tailcoat. But he was, you see, and so Alice had no choice but to take notice. 'O, Rabbit!' she cried, 'what is your name?'

Down the Brexit-hole

He stopped and turned to face her. 'David Camerabbit,' he replied, 'though you can call me Dave.' Then, twitching his nose, he reached inside his mustard-yellow waistcoat, pulled out a pocket watch and cried, 'I'm late! I'm late!'

'Late for what?' asked Alice.

'A very important date,' said the Rabbit, 'the twenty-third of June, to be precise. I need to appease my backbenchers, you see. Placate the Eurosceptics!'

And with that he went dashing off across a field. Alice, who was nothing if not curious, ran after him, as fast as her legs would carry her.

She ran and ran, then vaulted over a hedge, only to find her quarry waiting beside a rabbit-hole. The Camerabbit drew himself up and put on his best speech-giving voice. 'I believe with all my heart,' he said, 'in the will of the people. As such, I see no option but to resolve the debate over our national interest by jumping in this hole.' He then sprang forward and disappeared from view, leaving Alice in a quandary.

She was, at heart, a sensible girl, and knew it was rarely very wise to go jumping down holes with no knowledge of where they might lead. Yet there had been something in the Rabbit's tone – rich

4

and commanding, as though he had attended only the finest rabbit schools – that persuaded Alice she ought to just do it. And so, with a shrug of her shoulders, she leapt headfirst down the Brexit-hole…

Down, down, down Alice went, through a tunnel that soon widened to a vortex. Around her swirled a hurricane of ballot papers, French cheese and stingy Toblerones. Nick Robinson floated by, waving his arms and declaring that the laws of political gravity no longer applied. Beneath the whoosh of the air, she seemed to hear a nonsensical babbling, which spoke of 'Remoaners' and 'Bregret'.

By this point, Alice realised that she had been falling for a good ten minutes (though, personally, she would have deemed them a rather bad ten minutes). 'How long must I plummet?' she asked herself. 'If I don't land somewhere soon, it shall be getting past teatime. And what if I were to carry on through to the other side of the world? Should I find myself in the Antipodes, where up is down, day is night and a barbecue is a cultural event?'

It struck Alice that all this plummeting would be easier to tolerate if only Dinah were there. A cat, after all, could show her how to land upon her feet. She had just begun to wonder whether Australian cats

always landed on their heads, when – WHUMPH! – she hit the ground.

Alice was not a bit hurt. Picking herself up, she saw that she was in a tunnel, and that her fall had been broken by a large pile of papers. Looking closer, she found that each was a separate EU regulation. Being a free-spirited little girl, Alice was no fan of regulations, but she had to concede that these had proved vital to her health and safety.

Alice walked along the tunnel until she found herself in a strange hall, whose walls were lined with doors. These were black and numbered one to ten. She tried each in turn, but all of them were locked. Suddenly she came upon a three-legged table made of glass, upon which stood a newspaper. Attached to it was a label that said 'READ ME'. Alice was unsure whether this meant the paper or just the label, so decided she would read both to be on the safe side. She saw from the paper's red top that it was called the *Daily Murdoch*. On its front page ran the following words.

> *Beware the Eurocrat, old mate!*
> *His tape of red, his greedy paws*
> *He'll make all your bananas straight*
> *So say, 'Up yours, Delors!'*

Alice in Brexitland

He'll bind you with his Krautish rules
His kilos and his human rights
In fact, he and his frog's-leg fools
Cause all of Blighty's blights

He's why a horde of Turks and Poles
Steal jobs from Pete and Trevor
He's why your team just missed that goal
And why we have this weather

The fact you're sad and unemployed
Your kids don't want to see you
The time you had those haemorrhoids
It's all cos of the EU

O, British bloke! Despite all that
You've one trick still inside your sleeve
For you can slay the Eurocrat
Just cast your vote for Leave

Thus at the top of every lung
We'll tell the world to go to hell
Why should we learn another tongue
Or even ours, that well?

And then we'll breathe pure British air
As Blighty shines in all her charm
And if an Aussie billionaire
Should profit, where's the harm?

'Well now!' said Alice. 'I had no idea the EU was as bad as all that! It's a wonder that anyone stands for it.' As she read on (pausing to frown at the photograph on page three) Alice found herself growing more and more angry. The nerve of these Eurocrats! It said right there, in black and white, that they had banned the phrase 'best of British luck'. Henceforth, any luck wished would have to be in metric units, and of unspecified national origin. 'I don't pay tax,' said Alice, 'so that some Brussels-based pencil-pusher can tell me what to do. As a matter of fact, I don't pay tax at all!'

Being so very vexed, Alice failed to notice something remarkable: as her anger grew, so too did her stature. She shot up to five foot, then ten foot, then fifteen, until soon she filled the entire hall…

Chapter II

Furiouser and Furiouser

BANG! Alice's head hit the ceiling and she dropped her tabloid in fright. She found herself stooping, then kneeling, yet still there was barely enough room for her. Eventually she was forced to lie flat on her stomach, with an arm pinned behind her back and one foot up the chimney. With all that Alice had read, it seemed natural to assume that the EU was behind this transformation. 'How horrid!' she cried. 'Not only are atrocities being committed against the British banana, but now I have a crick in my neck!'

Turning her head as far as she could manage, Alice scanned the room for any item that might be of help. Her search did not take long, for lying outside the nearest door was another newspaper. This one, saw Alice, was called the *Gordian*. By squinting her eyes, she was just about able to read its tiny print. On the front page was a column calling for Britain to vote Remain.

It argued that, while the European Union had its fair share of flaws, it was ultimately a force for good in the world, despite the lurid claims bandied about by such organs as the *Daily Murdoch*. Alice found reading the *Gordian* very reassuring (although its tone *was* a little smug). As her temper cooled, she felt herself shrink down – fifteen foot, then ten foot, then five – until she had returned to her former height.

Although back to normal, Alice felt herself too much puzzled. Was the EU a devil, as depicted in the *Daily Murdoch*? Or was it the angel to be found in the pages of the *Gordian*? Perhaps it could be either, depending on who was looking at it. 'But then,' said Alice, 'how can I be sure that I am me? I may very well go calling myself Alice, when another would call me Ada, or Florence, or Gertrude. No, this is silly, for I know my name to be —' With a jolt of horror, she realised she had quite forgotten. Given how queer things had been today, it seemed no stretch to think she might have woken up as one person and now be another entirely.

'Enough of this!' thought Alice. 'I shall simply remember my lessons, then work my way back to who I am. Let me see: one times one is two... Two plus two is tutu... Buy one, get one three... Oh dear, that all seems wrong! Well, multiplication can be divisive, I'll try geography. The capital of Rome is London. London is the capital of Paris. But then I'm sure the capital of London is "L"… Oh, geography's no good either. I'll try and say "How Doth the Politician".'

How doth the politician lie
To burnish his career
And with his bogus slogans try
To bend the voter's ear!

He'll promise in each interview
That perfect joy awaits
And all the while he's screwing you
To help his wealthy mates

This did not sound quite right to Alice (especially the part about screwing). Just then, the White Rabbit came running towards her. 'O, Rabbit!' cried Alice, 'you must help me! I've no idea what's going on!' In spite of his large, floppy ears, the creature did not seem to hear her, for he made no sign of stopping. Rather, he bounded up to door number ten and, as he ducked inside, Alice could hear the Rabbit hum a merry tune and murmur the word 'good!' She ran after him and banged her little fists against the door. 'Dave!' she yelled, 'I followed you down this hole; the least you can do is help me out of it!'

When came there no reply, poor Alice felt her eyes well up with tears. 'That awful Rabbit!' she sobbed. 'I thought he knew what he was talking about, but really he was just posh!' The more she dwelled on it, the more she cried, and soon a salty puddle had formed beneath her. This puddle grew into a pool, and then a river, and Alice was swept along, swimming against the tide.

Eventually, a great wave deposited her upon the shore. While relieved not to have been drowned, Alice was soaked through, and felt quite miserable. Fortunately, among some nearby reeds, there was a radio broadcasting a speech by George Galloway. Faced with such a tremendous blast of hot air, it took mere seconds for Alice's clothes to dry out.

This problem resolved, she was free to explore her surroundings. Before her stood a forest and, wandering through it, Alice noted that the leaves of each tree had written on them either 'IN' or 'OUT'. Soon she came upon a clearing, where a large group of woodland creatures were engaged in what is euphemistically known as a 'spirited debate'.

The discussion seemed to revolve primarily around two figures: a fox and a hedgehog.

'Vote Leave!' said the fox.

'Remain!' said the hedgehog.

'I'm undecided,' said a mouse.

The hedgehog called the fox a fascist. The fox replied by saying that the hedgehog was part of a metropolitan elite.

A duck muttered darkly about how he worked every day, and did not want his bread going to some fancy mallard in Spain. Many of the other animals looked weary and forlorn, as though they wished to God they had never started this debate.

'We've opened a can of worms,' said the badger.

'What? WHERE?!' said the sparrow.

Alice approached a vole who stood on the outskirts of the group.

'Pray tell,' she said, 'who are the creatures gathered here?'

'We call ourselves the General Public,' said the vole, 'for we only know things in general and have no grasp of detail.'

'And what,' said Alice, 'is the cause of all this tumult?'

'Why,' he replied, 'the referendum, of course!'

The fox continued to dominate proceedings. 'This country,' he said, 'is a proud democracy – the mother of all democracies – and we cannot afford to surrender our decision-making to faceless foreign bureaucrats.'

'He's got a point,' said the mouse.

'Thanks mate!' said the fox. 'You seem a good, decent bloke, you should come back to my den sometime.'

'Don't listen to him!' warned the hedgehog. 'He just wants to eat you!'

'Typical Project Fear,' said the fox.

'Look,' said the cock, 'the fact is, we need to clamp down on immigration.'

'Here we go again!' sighed the hedgehog, rolling her eyes. 'Whenever one attempts to have a civilised debate, some cock starts banging on about immigrants.'

'All I'm saying,' the cock continued, 'is that we don't want foreigners flooding into our forest and changing our way of life. This vote is an opportunity to take back control and tell the frogs to get stuffed!'

'What've we done to deserve that?' said the frog.

'Apologies,' said the cock. 'Of course, I was merely referring to Frenchmen. And, given what they do to the likes of you, you ought to sympathise.'

'You want to talk about facts?' said the hedge-hog. 'Here are some facts: immigration to the forest is going down, not up. On top of that, immigrants pay more into the economy that they take out. Also, we're heavily dependent on exports, which is why every leading economist says Brexit would reduce our GDP by up to fifteen per cent.'

'Those may be *your* facts,' said the cock, 'but we have our own set of facts and they're every bit as true.'

Alice felt more confused than ever. Plucking up her courage, she strode into the middle of the assembly.

'Excuse me,' Alice said, in the most grown-up voice she could muster, 'perhaps you fine creatures could explain the cause of your quarrel. I'm new here, you see.'

'New?' said the fox, with a suspicious look. 'How did you come to be in this forest?'

'I swam here,' said Alice.

'Swam here?' said the fox, now baring his teeth. 'So you're an immigrant! An *illegal* immigrant!'

'Oh, don't be like that,' said Alice, 'for I've had such a difficult time. I had to swim for miles and miles. I might well have drowned!'

'And it would have served you right!' said the cock. 'You're probably a criminal, or worse, a health tourist!'

'Bloody little girls,' said the duck, 'coming over here and stealing our jobs.'

'I don't want your beastly job!' said Alice, taken aback. 'In fact, I've never had a job in my life.'

'SHE'S ON BENEFITS!' cried the cock, and almost fell off his perch, such was his excitement.

By now the crowd had become quite mutinous and Alice could hear shouts of, 'Go back to where you came from!' and 'British jobs for British workers!' The geese were booing and the snakes all hissed. Alice sensed the popular mood had turned against her. 'I stand with you,' whispered the hedgehog, backing away. Alice thought it might be wise to make a retreat, and so she did, wandering deeper and deeper into the forest.

Chapter III

Advice from the Corbyn-pillar

After not too long a spell of trudging, Alice happened upon a huge, red mushroom, larger than any she had previously encountered. Once she had looked under it, and on both sides of it, and behind it, it occurred to her that she might as well look and see what was on top of it. So she stretched herself up on tiptoe, and peeped over the edge. Her eyes immediately met those of a large, red caterpillar, who wore a Lenin cap, an ill-fitting suit and a permanently bored expression. He was sitting on top of the mushroom, with his arms folded, quietly smoking a long hookah and taking not the smallest notice of her or anything else.

Eventually, the Caterpillar took the hookah out of his mouth and addressed Alice in a languid, sleepy voice.

'Who are *you*?' said the Caterpillar.

'I'm not quite sure who I am,' said Alice. 'I might have given you a definite answer this morning, but the world has grown so queer since then, I fear I could be anyone.'

The Caterpillar puffed on his pipe, not at all impressed.

'You must be someone,' he said, 'otherwise you would be some-*none*, and it would hardly be worth my while talking to you.'

'If I am someone,' said Alice, 'then I am someone very confused. Ever since I went down the Brexit-hole, I have had this tremendous pain in my head, and facts and figures, truth and lies, they all seem jumbled up. I've even started to forget things.'

'What sort of things?' said the Caterpillar.

'Well, I tried to say a poem, but it all came out different,' Alice replied in a very melancholy voice.

'Try another one,' said the Caterpillar. 'Recite "Mr Corbyn".'

Alice folded her hands, and began,

'You are crap, Mr Corbyn,' the MP said
'And I don't want to face deselection
But the polls have the Tories five hundred ahead
How the hell can we win an election?'

Advice from the Corbyn-pillar

Alice in Brexitland

'Dear comrade,' replied Mr Corbyn, 'those polls
Are wrong – did you not get the memo?
Just focus instead on the thousands of souls
Who flock to my every last demo'

'You are crap,' said the member, his nose out of joint
'Have you even been watching the news?
They say you're a joke and they did have a point
When you nodded off in PMQs'

'My plan,' said the sage, as he stroked his white beard
'Is to look both inept and unwise
And once I have been universally jeered
I'll take Number Ten by surprise'

'You are crap,' said the MP, with anguish sincere
'May's awful – we need you to finish her
You say you want change, but still it's unclear
That you care about being prime minister'

'This slander,' said Jeremy, 'makes us feel sad'
(Note his use of the monarchist 'we')
'Though I disobeyed every leader I've had
I demand your complete loyalty'

Advice from the Corbyn-pillar

'You are crap and you're pushing us over the brink
So I must resign!' cried the MP
And now although Labour's in need of a drink
They find that their cabinet's empty

'Well, that settles that,' Corbyn said to himself
As he sat on the front bench alone
And while the Conservatives privatised health
He smiled at the strength that he'd shown

The Caterpillar stared at Alice. For a moment, she worried she might have offended him in some way. However, he simply took a long drag on his pipe, then murmured, 'That was wrong from beginning to end.'

There was silence for some minutes. Eventually, Alice felt the need to break it.

'Excuse me, Caterpillar,' she said, 'what is your job?'

'I suppose I'm meant to oppose the government,' he replied, 'but I prefer to sit here all day, feeling self-righteous.'

'You're a politician?' said Alice, who saw a chance to clear things up. 'Then you must know all about the referendum. Tell me, are you in favour of the European Union?'

The Caterpillar did not say a word; he just sat there, puffing on his hookah.

'I'm sorry, did you not hear me?' said Alice. 'I asked what you thought of the EU.'

'E who?' said the Caterpillar, blowing a smoke ring. Alice frowned.

'It's hardly an unreasonable question,' she said.

With a sigh, the Caterpillar took the pipe out of his mouth.

'I'd rate it seven,' he said, 'or seven-and-a-half out of ten.'

This struck Alice as a most unsatisfactory answer, and so she turned to leave.

'Wait!' the Caterpillar called after her. 'I've something important to say.'

This sounded promising, certainly. Alice turned and came back again.

'Do you like my mushroom?' said the Caterpillar.

'Is that all?' said Alice, swallowing down her anger as well as she could.

'It's big and red,' he continued, 'and special power lies within it. If you eat a piece from the left side, you become a hero of the proletariat. However, if you eat a piece from the right, it turns you into Blairite scum.'

With this, a shade fell across his features.

'What,' asked Alice, 'is a Blairite?' (For it sounded a fearful creature.)

'The Blairites are our mortal enemy,' the Caterpillar replied, 'they would compromise our party's ideals in order to win elections.'

'Forgive me,' said Alice, 'but if they're in your party, how can they be your mortal enemy? Surely that title is reserved for the party you oppose?'

'Don't be stupid,' the Caterpillar said. 'Blairites are the vilest thing on earth. If I suspect a person to be one, I have them chased from the forest by my Momentums.'

Alice was beginning to think she had had quite enough of the Caterpillar.

'So, if I understand correctly,' she said, 'you sit around all day bemoaning a government whose actions you can't be bothered to oppose, you spend most of your energy picking fights with your own party and when voters ask your opinion on the most important question facing Britain today, you'd rather do anything than give a straight answer?'

'Pretty much,' the Caterpillar replied.

'What kind of a leader are you?' cried Alice. 'If you really wanted to help people, you'd get off your backside and try and win power!'

The Caterpillar let the hookah drop from his lips, and his face changed from its usual red to an even angrier shade. He reared up to his full height of three inches, threw his head back and let out a deafening cry: 'BLAIRIIIIIIIIIITE!'

Alice heard the sound of a thousand footsteps behind her. Out of the trees, whooping and hollering, came a horde of Momentums. Beholding their fiery eyes and flaring nostrils, Alice had no doubt that they wished to tear her limb from limb. With a yelp, she ran in the opposite direction, and the Momentums chased after her, shouting 'Blairite scum!' and 'Red Tory!'

Eventually, Alice rounded a corner and came to the edge of a cliff. Had she not her wits about her, she would almost certainly have tumbled off. Hiding behind a nearby tree, she looked across, only to see her pursuers running right towards the cliff's edge. Alice jumped out and tried to warn them, but the Momentums had too much momentum to stop. As they fell to their certain deaths, Alice could still hear, carried on the wind, faint cries of 'Red Tory!' and 'Blairite scum!'

Chapter IV

The Cheshire Twat

Alice now found herself in the deepest, darkest reaches of the forest. As she looked around, she saw the trees had grown into strange, twisted shapes, and shook their branches in a sinister fashion. One tree in particular caught Alice's eye. It was a gaudy-looking thing, with purple and yellow leaves, and a great pound sign carved upon its trunk. As she drew closer, Alice was startled to see, perched on one of its boughs, a large cat. She would not normally have been startled to see a cat, except that this one had a huge grin on its face and was taking swigs from a pint glass. It looked good-natured, Alice thought. Still, it had *very* long claws and a great many teeth.

'O, Cat!' cried Alice. 'Why do you smile so wide?'

'Why shouldn't I?' he replied. 'I'm having a bloody British beer in the middle of the day, and there's nothing the PC brigade can do to stop me.'

Alice frowned. Despite the Cat's smiling face, he had a malign air about him.

'Who are the PC brigade?' asked Alice. 'Are they some kind of constabulary?'

'I don't know about the "abulary",' the Cat replied, 'but they're certainly the first part. The PC brigade are a bunch of loony lefties who tell ordinary, decent people that they're not allowed to say what they think.'

'Well then,' said Alice, 'my governess must be a member; she tells me to be quiet whenever I speak my mind. For instance, the time I told Mabel that her new dress looked rotten. Is that the sort of thing they don't like you saying?'

But the Cat just smiled and took another sip.

'It's been ever such an odd day,' said Alice. 'I'm lost, you see, and if I don't find my way soon, I fear I shall go mad.'

The Cat grinned a little wider.

'Oh, I shouldn't worry about that,' he said. 'We're all mad here. I've gone mad, you've gone mad, political correctness has gone mad…'

'It's funny you should mention politics,' said Alice, 'for I'm ever so confused about the current situation. Oh! Perhaps *you* could help me. I need to

make up my mind regarding the EU.'

At this, the Cat's grin became so wide, it almost joined at the back of his head.

'I'd be only too happy to oblige,' he said.

'Wonderful,' said Alice. 'I tried asking the Caterpillar, but he was quite useless.'

'Yes, a lot of people come to me from him,' said the Cat. 'Now, let me start by saying, I am the EU's greatest enemy. I have spent my life fighting it and I have eight more lives with which to do

31

so. But I am glad of this fight, for our country will never be free until it casts off the yoke of Brussels. We need to take back control – British laws for British people. Just look at border security. All we want is a commonsense approach to immigration. Of course, saying that makes me racist, if you listen...' – and here his voice grew dark – '...to *them*.'

'Them?' said Alice.

'Yes,' said the Cat. 'Y'know... Them...'

'I don't know,' said Alice. 'Perhaps you could specify who "they" are?'

'They,' said the Cat, 'are *them*. Those people. The ones who go around, doing *that sort of thing*.'

'I have no idea what you mean,' said Alice, becoming rather frustrated.

The Cat ploughed on regardless.

'The thing about *them*,' he said, 'is they're ruining this country. This is no longer the land I loved as a kitten. Great Britain used to be Great, but now it's all "safe space" this and "trigger warning" that and one can barely move for sexual harassment tribunals! Hmm, perhaps there's a better way for me to explain...'

At this point, the Cat put his drink to one side and burst into song,

The Cheshire Twat

How I long for the olden days, golden and gay
When posties would whistle and bid you good day
When folks were polite, wouldn't dare make a fuss
And no one spoke Polish while riding the bus

The land of the hedgerow, the spinney and fen
Of gooseberries and sponge cakes and uncles
    called Ken
Where ruddy-faced fellows drove funny old cars
And birds didn't mind a bloke slapping their arse

We'd never ask questions; we knew all the answers
We liked Morris Minors and loved Morris dancers
And bullshit like bulldogs, John Bull, bully beef
And never acknowledging beauty or grief

The White Cliffs of Dover, the National Trust
Spitfires, evensong, B. Windsor's bust
The hats worn at Ascot – keep calm, carry on! –
The Bible and blackface and eating a swan

Steeples and cobblestones, banter and cheer
Elgar and Churchill and warm, English beer
We'd raise up our flagons and toast to the Queen
Then talk about all of the totty we'd seen

*And people took pride in their strong, English
     names
Like Blenkinsop, Robinson, Jenkins and James
That's just how we liked them, although, by and
     large,
We didn't mind Huguenot names like 'Farage'*

*I'm smitten with Britain, the way it was then
When women were women and men could be men
For life was quite marvellous back in the day
(Unless you were African, Jewish or gay)*

As soon as the Cat had finished, he downed the
remainder of his pint, and Alice was amazed to see it
magically fill back up. She had not much enjoyed his
song, for many of its words were unfamiliar. Nonetheless, it seemed clear to Alice that this Cat did not
like the world, and so preferred to live in one that
never really existed.

The Cat pulled out a pack of Benson & Hedges,
removed the wrapper with his claws, then stuck one
in his mouth and lit up. Alice was glad she had never
seen Dinah, her own cat, behave in this manner.

'Ah, that takes the edge off,' said the Cat, exhal-
ing. 'I love my ciggies. Scientists tell you they cause

cancer, but everyone knows science is run by our *Hebrew* friends…. Of course, you're not allowed to say that anymore.'

'Hmm, yes, to be sure,' said Alice, feeling somewhat depressed.

It seemed to Alice that the Cat was constantly saying things that he claimed were forbidden, and yet no penalty seemed forthcoming. 'Alas,' she said, with a sigh, 'everything in this place is so terribly queer.'

'What's that about queers?' exclaimed the Cat, dropping his cigarette.

'Oh no,' said Alice, 'I mean "queer" as in "strange", "out-of-the-way".'

'I should bloody well hope so,' said the Cat, then vanished.

Before Alice could properly take this in, she found that the Cat had reappeared behind her. 'You know,' he said, 'it's not just Blighty that's gone mad. Everywhere's topsy-turvy at the moment: Wop Country, Frogsylvania, Bongo Bongo Land. And, as for the States… You know, I happen to be flying over there for a speaking engagement – those Yanks have deep pockets. I could take you along, if you'd like? Just hop on my back.'

Alice was hesitant; the Cat has used so many phrases that made her feel uncomfortable. However, for want of anything better to do, she decided to climb aboard. Politics aside, a free flight was a free flight.

'Mind the pint!' he said, as she drew up her legs and settled on his back.

Within moments, they were floating twenty feet above the forest floor, and veering wildly from side to side. Alice began to wonder if this journey was wise, given how much the Cat had had to drink.

'Perhaps I should wear a seatbelt,' said Alice.

'Seatbelts,' said the Cat, 'are for poofters.'

Then, with a belch, he shot up through the treetops. The Cat flew Alice away from the forest, across miles of rolling countryside, until soon they were over the vast Atlantic ocean...

Chapter V

A Mad Tea Party

It was a long, turbulent flight, and, during the course of it, the Cheshire Cat was sick several times. Eventually, however, they came to land in the faraway realm of Middle America (or, rather, it *had* been faraway; now they were there it was extremely close).

'Whew,' said the Cat, 'that was a smoother landing than I'm used to.' On one side of them was a prairie and, on the other, a cornfield that stretched as far as the eye could see. Alice had no idea which state they were in, but she imagined it had an exotic name, something like 'Texachussetts' or 'Nebrucky'.

'Ah, America,' said the Cheshire Cat. 'Like all patriotic Brits, I would absolutely love to live here. Now, let's—'

Suddenly, he fell quiet, for they could hear cries across the plain; peculiar cries, such as 'WOO-HOO!', 'YEE-HAW!' and 'LOCK HER UP!'

Alice and the Cat followed these voices until they reached a field that was dotted with tables, barbecues, tilt-a-whirls, shooting galleries and mechanical bulls. Everywhere Alice turned there were Americans running around in mad hats: tricornes and stovepipes and toppers. However, the maddest hats that Alice saw were red baseball caps, emblazoned with the words 'MAKE AMERICA GREAT AGAIN'.

'Who are these Mad Hatters?' she asked, only to find that her companion had disappeared. It was not at all fun to be abandoned in a strange country – or, indeed, a bizarre one – but Alice was a resilient young lady, and so she decided to approach the refreshment stand. As she loaded up on tater tots and deep-fried Oreos, she found herself accosted by a hare. He was six-foot tall, wore a bolo tie, and sounded exactly like Matthew McConaughey.

40

'Well, howdy,' drawled the Hare, 'what's your name, sugar?'

'Alice,' she said, then added, 'are you a March hare?'

'Naw,' he replied, 'I'm more of a Ju-ly Fourth kind of hare.'

'Pleased to meet you,' said Alice. 'What are all these people doing here?'

'Why, this is the Mad Tea Party,' said the Hare. 'It's only the merriest, most right-wing gathering of the year!'

'Oh, a tea party!' said Alice. 'How wonderful! Might I trouble you for a cup of Earl Grey?'

'No can do, darlin',' said the Hare, 'we *had* tea, but we done threw it all in the harbour. We got a buttload of beers, though.'

Alice declined as politely as she could.

'Suit yourself,' he replied. 'I'd better get back to my buddies on the main table. Feel free to come join us.'

So Alice sat down at the table, which was piled high with hotdogs and burgers, meatloaf and ribs. The Hare sat beside her, munching on a hoagie and chugging a can of Budweiser. Alice looked about at the assembled guests. There were hundreds and hundreds of faces, but not a single one was black. This was so obvious that even Alice, a girl from Victorian England, could not help but notice. She considered asking the Hare why all of his friends were white, but soon thought better of it.

'Excuse me,' said Alice, 'but if there's no tea to be had, what makes this a tea party?'

'Little lady, I'm glad you asked. You see, this land is ruled by a Muslim by the name of *Obama*.' He spat out the name as though he had accidentally eaten a vegetable. 'We're gathered here today because we hate the man with all our hearts. He is, without a doubt, the greatest sinner who ever lived.'

'What has he done?' asked Alice.

'What *hasn't* he done?' said the Hare. 'First off, he uses long, confusing words in his speeches, words like "democracy" and "healthcare". Second off, his skin is entirely the wrong colour. It's confusing as heck to see the guy in charge lookin' like that.'

'That certainly does sound…' said Alice, but was unsure how to finish.

'Don't you worry, though,' said the Hare, 'cause we gon' be just fine. At long last, a man has come to lead us. A true champion of the people, who wants to make America great again!'

'Ah,' thought Alice, 'so that explains those ugly baseball caps…'

'Oh, yes indeedy doody,' continued the Hare, 'America shall be great again and the South shall rise!'

'Be careful it doesn't rise too far,' said Alice, 'for then it would be the North.'

The Hare, who did not seem to appreciate this advice, merely wrinkled his nose and returned to his hoagie. Alice was about to ask the name of their new leader, when a band began to play and the whole group leapt to its feet for a hoedown.

(To the tune of 'Yankee Doodle')

Obama ain't our president
Cos he was born in Kenya
Which is in the Middle East
As far as we remember

CHORUS:
Yankees do not care for facts
Just the things we reckon
Number one we love our flags
And snacking comes in second

We get all our news from Fox
Cos they are always truthful
Did you know that Hillary
Eats babies to stay youthful?

Alice in Brexitland

(CHORUS)

Muslims want to blow you up
And Mexicans are lazy
Or is that the wrong way round?
It's all a little hazy

(CHORUS)

Blacks complain they have it hard
But we just tell 'em 'save it!'
They came here to steal our jobs
All cosy on their slave ships

(CHORUS)

Don't you tell us that our guns
Could put our kids in danger
We wish Jesus had a Glock
To play with in the manger

(CHORUS)

(Solemn)
Sometimes we feel dead inside

A Mad Tea Party

As though our hearts are failin'
(Cheerful and fast)
Then we think of flags and snacks
And good old Sarah Palin!

(CHORUS x 2, all singers throw up)

Alice surveyed the devastation this mad dance had caused. Some of the revellers had jumped up on the table, trampling their food and smashing their plates. Some had even jumped onto their barbecues and been horribly burned. As bewildering as Brexitland could be, it was nothing compared to this place. Alice thought it extraordinary that these people should share a language with her, when their attitude to life was so different.

'I hope you don't mind me saying,' began Alice, in a tone of grave reproof, 'but I don't think one ought to go around disliking people due to the colour of their skin.'

Instead of responding, the Hare leapt up on the table and yelled a phrase, to which the group responded without missing a beat:

'What do we like?'

'Pretzels and hot sauce and foam hands and trucks!'

'What DON'T we like?'

'Libtards and eggheads and A-rabs and cucks!'

The Hare sat back down, looking much pleased with himself.

'I'm not sure you heard me,' said Alice, 'but, again, I think you're being dreadfully unfair to your Mr Obama.'

'I don't give a damn what you think, limey,' the Hare replied. 'That's why we had the original Tea Party: to take back control. We left the British Empire in what became known as Brempexit.'

Suddenly, all the charm had vanished from his Matthew McConaughey voice.

'Well, it's getting late,' said Alice. 'I should head off… It looks as though the party's winding down.'

'Oh no, darlin',' said the Hare, with an icy tone, 'this party's just getting started…'

Alice looked around her, for there had been a change in the atmosphere. The revellers no longer laughed and shouted 'WOO-HOO!', but rather muttered darkly and reached underneath their chairs. Alice's blood ran cold when she saw them putting on a different kind of hat: tall, white, pointy ones, complete with eyeholes. She heard a sudden WHOOSH! and turned to see a group of white hat-wearers setting fire to a cross. This was all too much for Alice, and so she got up, ran away from the table and tore through the cornfields as fast as she could. Such was Alice's haste that she forgot to look where she was going and – CLANG! – ran headfirst into a wall. Not just any wall, mind you: a wall made of solid gold. Picking herself off the ground, Alice was overwhelmed by a repugnant, eggy stench. She looked up to see, perched atop the golden wall, none other than Trumpty Dumpty.

Chapter VI

Trumpty Dumpty

This creature was more peculiar than any Alice had yet encountered. He was not fully an egg, nor could you say he was quite a man, but somehow existed in between the two states. He had orange skin, squinty eyes and a puckered little mouth that reminded Alice of her cat's bottom. On top of all this lay a thatch of golden hair, much the same colour as Alice's, but of a texture that she had never seen before. In his hands he held a smartphone, whose screen he jabbed with stubby fingers. He seemed as angry as an egg could be, unless it were actually boiling in water, and, as he jabbed, strange words burbled from his lips.

'Horrible... Bigly... Alec Baldwin... SAD!'

This piqued Alice's interest all the more.

'Excuse me,' she said, 'but my name is Alice and —'

'Shut up!' cried the Egg. 'I'm tweeting.'

A tweeting egg! This struck Alice as very odd; she had only ever heard of birds being able to tweet. But, then again, birds *did* come from eggs, so it made sense they should have this ability from the outset. After a while, the Egg sat back and sighed, content.

'OK,' he said, 'I've attacked a TV show, told my followers to harass a dying child and retweeted some guy called NaziBoy88 – a good day's work.'

52

As he spoke to himself, Alice noticed something odd: the golden wall, while very tall, extended only a few feet from side to side. One could walk around it without much effort at all.

'Excuse me, sir,' said Alice, 'but what's the use of a wall that doesn't connect to anything?'

The Egg finally took notice, and peered down at her, annoyed.

'Listen,' he said, 'this is a big, beautiful wall – everybody says so. I have the best wall, the classiest wall, made of real gold. It's gonna stretch for a million miles and Mexico is gonna pay for it, believe me.'

Here, he pursed up his lips, and looked so solemn and grand that Alice could hardly help laughing.

'Pray tell, what is your wall *for*?' asked Alice.

'To keep the Mexicans out,' replied the Egg.

'But sir,' said Alice, rather doubtfully, 'why then would they pay for it? Surely, if Mexicans wished to be kept out, they would simply not come in the first place. It seems rather a roundabout method to go buying themselves a wall.'

'WRONG!' yelled the Egg, turning from orange to bright red. 'They will pay for it because I'm so good at business. Believe me, I'm the richest egg in the world – way richer than those Fabergé losers –

and if you say any different, I'll sue you so hard your head will spin!'

'Goodness,' thought Alice, 'this egg has such a thin shell and his hands are so *very* small.'

Alice was finding the company of this loud-mouthed Egg-man far from pleasant. She felt an urge to return to Brexitland, whose strangeness was at least more familiar. To do that, she would need to locate the Cheshire Cat.

'Have you seen a pussy?' she asked.

'If I had,' the Egg replied, 'I would've grabbed it, believe me.'

Alice didn't quite understand what this meant, but it made her feel sad and not a little sick. (Although that may have been, in part, his sulphurous smell.)

'So,' barked the Egg, 'what have you got me?'

'Got you?' said Alice, not at all sure what was going on.

'Are you an idiot?' he said. 'I mean, what present have you got me for my un-birthday?'

'I'm afraid I have no present, sir,' said Alice, 'and, I must confess, I've never heard of an *un*-birthday. In my country, we merely celebrate one's birthday.'

'Birthdays are for losers,' replied the Egg. 'You only get one a year. Sad, horrible. I celebrate the three hundred and sixty-four days when it's *not* my birthday. That's three hundred and sixty-four gift-giving opportunities for the people who love me.'

'And who are they?' asked Alice.

There followed a long pause. It seemed Alice had touched upon a sore spot, so she decided to move the conversation along.

'Tell me, sir,' she began, 'where do you stand on the EU referendum?'

'I don't stand on any referendum,' he shot back, 'I sit on this wall. Are you blind as well as stupid?'

'So you have no feelings on Brexit?' said Alice.

'Oh, Brexit!' exclaimed the Egg, seemingly cheered. 'I love Brexit. They call me Mr Brexit.'

A silly thought popped into Alice's mind, as silly thoughts were wont to do. 'If a British exit is a Brexit,' said Alice, 'is a bird's hatching an egg-xit?'

To Alice's alarm, the creature's eyes narrowed further, and his cat's-bottom mouth puckered more.

'Is that a threat?' he growled. 'You want to see me crack and a bird come out? Listen, sweetheart, I know guys in the KGB who could make you disappear like *that*.'

On this last word, the Egg snapped his fingers, but they were so tiny that no sound could be heard.

'Well, really!' said Alice. 'It was nothing but a harmless joke.'

'I don't find jokes funny,' replied the Egg. 'In fact, I'm not capable of feeling any joy whatsoever. I guess it's because my mommy didn't love me.'

It occurred to Alice that Trumpty Dumpty must be quite a sad egg, really.

'I'm sorry your mother didn't love you,' she said.

'What?!' he yelled in outrage. 'My mom loved me more than anything in the world! No one has ever said any different!'

'But you just told me she didn't,' said Alice.

'That's a lie!' he cried. 'Your reporting is horrible! Such a nasty little girl!'

Alice glared at the self-involved ovum, for his rudeness was quite appalling. Nonetheless, she thought she would make one last attempt to reason with him.

'You know,' she said, 'you can't go around saying one thing one minute, then the opposite the next. Words do have meaning.'

'When I use a word,' he replied in rather a scornful tone, 'and, by the way, I use the best words, the most luxurious words, it means just what I choose it to mean.'

'The question is,' said Alice, 'whether you can make words mean so many different things.'

'I can do what I want,' he said, 'always have done, always will. From now on, I'm gonna call you Crooked Alice. And if you don't watch your mouth, I'll have you thrown in jail.'

Alice frowned darkly at the Egg. She found herself hoping that he would have a great fall in the very near future.

As she thought this, Alice was surprised to see the Cheshire Cat, who had reappeared at the top of the wall. He proceeded to lick and nuzzle Trumpty Dumpty's shell, as though trying to win his approval. The Cat nuzzled and licked ever more frantically as he went on, to the point that Alice worried where all of this would lead. But the Egg seemed not to notice and returned to his tweeting.

'Fake news,' he murmured, 'Obamacare. Yuuuuuuge.'

Alice, now firmly convinced that the Egg before her was the worst and most rancid in the whole wide world, decided to give him a piece of her mind:

'Of all the unsatisfactory people I have *ever* met —'

Just then, the Egg unleashed an almighty trump, a gust of such magnitude that it swept Alice off her feet and hurled her across the Atlantic, all the way back to Brexitland.

Chapter VII

Tweedleboz and Tweedlegove

Fortunately, Alice's fall was broken – and nothing else – when she came to rest in a typical English town. Unfortunately, the object that had broken it was a large and ornate cake. 'Crumbs!' yelled the baker, dismayed to see his hard work go to waste.

'Kind sir,' said Alice, who was quite covered in icing, 'would you please tell me where I am?'

But he was in no mood to help her. 'Oh, I had baked that for the rally!' he cried. Railing at this new scourge of little girls falling from the sky, the baker stomped off down the lane, leaving Alice to examine her surroundings. In the town square stood a platform, around which was gathered a large group of creatures, chanting and waving signs. Soon Alice had pushed through to the front, where she found an angry branch, a fuming twig and a cross stick.

'Those EU bastards!' said the Branch. 'Did you know they want to paint the White Cliffs of Dover brown in case Muslims get offended?'

'Yes,' said the Twig, 'and they want to ban us from using our *Christian* names! I read about it in the *Daily Murdoch*.'

'Excuse me,' said Alice, 'what is this event in aid of?'

'Why, the Leave campaign, you ninny!' said the Stick. 'Now be quiet: they're about to speak.'

Alice looked across to see two strange fellows, each struggling to climb onstage. One had a deranged mop of blond hair; the other looked like a duck who had just won a prize.

'Who *are* those fat little men?' said Alice.

'Those,' said the Twig, 'are the brothers Twee-dleboz and Tweedlegove. They are the intellectual heavyweights of our campaign.'

'Really?' said Alice. 'They look so exactly like a couple of great schoolboys!'

With considerable difficulty, the brothers managed to roll across to the podium, where they stood a while, huffing and puffing. The blond-haired one spoke first.

'Ooh, ah, gosh, crikey. Ladies and gentlemen, believe me when I say the European Union is nothing

more than an odious blancmange. We cannot allow
ourselves to be dictated to by every Tomas, Ricardo
and Heinrich. Nohow!'

Next, the duck-faced one stepped forward.

'Contrariwise,' he said, 'leaving the EU would
afford our nation tremendous financial opportunities.
Now, so-called "experts" will say that's rubbish, and
that telling our largest trading partner to get stuffed

will inevitably damage our economy. However, I happen to believe that people in this country have had enough of experts.'

The speech went on for what seemed to Alice an eternity, especially as the brothers kept breaking off to hug one another. The rest of the audience, however, were entranced. Tweedlegove would say things that seemed awfully clever (for he wore glasses) and, whenever this threatened to become tiresome, Tweedleboz would jump in with a Latin pun, or a joke that was borderline racist.

Prompted, perhaps, by the sight of a blond charlatan, Alice's thoughts returned to Trumpty Dumpty. She pictured the Egg lying at the base of his wall, shattered into a thousand pieces. His pouty little mouth lay on the grass nearby, still burbling with outrage. 'How dare the crooked media say I've had a great fall?' exclaimed the mouth. 'Believe me, I'm the least cracked guy you've ever seen!' At this point, all the king's horses and all the king's men came along, but, rather than trying to put Trumpty together again, they instead jumped up and down on the pieces until there was nothing left.

Alice emerged from this pleasant daydream to find that the brothers were still speaking.

'Our participation in the Leave campaign is born of a deep, heartfelt conviction,' said Tweedleboz. 'A conviction that we have always held, for we are patriots first and politicians second.'

'Contrariwise,' said Tweedlegove, 'if choosing this side should happen to help our careers, that is a sacrifice we are willing to make.'

This was the longest Alice could remember going without speaking, and so she called up to the stage.

'Pray tell,' said Alice, 'what, specifically, are the economic advantages of Brexit?'

Tweedleboz and Tweedlegove both looked horribly alarmed.

'By Jingo!' said Tweedleboz. 'Lawks-a-mussy!'

'Little girl,' said Tweedlegove, 'I am very pleased you asked that question… Yes, our economy is frightfully important. Fundamentally, though, this debate is about asserting British values of decency, transparency and fairness. It's a matter of principle, and principles are more precious than money.'

'Hang on a minute,' said Alice, 'you spent the last hour arguing that Brexit will make us better off, but now you turn around and say this is about some vague principles. Which is it?'

There followed an awkward silence, during which the crowd seemed to grow unsettled. Finally, Tweedleboz stepped forward and, with an expression of the utmost solemnity, dropped his trousers to reveal a pair of bright yellow boxers. There was a palpable sense of relief as the whole crowd fell about laughing.

'LOL,' said the Branch, '*classic* Tweedleboz. That guy is a legend.'

'Good old Boz,' said the Twig, 'always getting into funny scrapes. Not like boring, *normal* politicians.'

'So the fact he behaves like a buffoon,' said Alice, 'is what makes you think he should be in charge?'

'Oh, don't be so politically correct,' said the Stick.

'People keep saying that,' thought Alice, 'but I scarcely know what they mean. Has it suddenly become a good thing to be incorrect? If so, I should remember that when I'm called upon to do my twelve-times table.'

Suddenly, the crowd parted and the White Rabbit came running through. 'The results are in!' he cried, his face even whiter than normal: 'IT'S BREXIT!'

The Leavers erupted in a deafening cheer, then began turning over tables and head-butting walls with delight.

'The public has voted to leave,' continued the Rabbit, 'fifty-two to forty-eight.'

'A LANDSLIDE!' cried the Leavers, upsetting apple-carts and setting fire to their hair.

'Well, that's that,' said the Rabbit. 'I've basically ruined everything for everyone. I suppose I'd better go home and play Fruit Ninja.' And so he hopped off, once again humming his jaunty little tune.

Although the crowd was overjoyed, Alice noted that Tweedleboz and Tweedlegove looked anything but. In fact, they were shaking all over, with great beads of sweat coursing down their faces. It was almost as though the pair of them had not been anticipating this result. As they hugged each other more tightly than ever, Alice could make out their whispered words.

TWEEDLEGOVE:
I'm shocked, I'm scared, I feel quite sick
My mouth's dry and my neck hurts!
O, why'm I such an awful prick?
I'd better ask some experts

TWEEDLEBOZ:
Have I got news for you: we're screwed!
The country won't recover

O, why'd they trust some porky dude
Who looks like Malfoy's brother?

A journalist crab scuttled onto the stage, holding a notebook in one claw and a pen in the other.

'Harold Pincer, the *Gordian*,' said the Crab. 'During the campaign, you promised extra funding for the NHS if Britain voted to leave. When can we expect to see it?'

Instead of replying, Tweedleboz and Tweedlegove began to dance around madly, and sing in unison,

We've lost control, we've gone too far, what will
become of us?
Instead of merely telling lies, we wrote them on a bus!
We said three hundred fifty mill a week, but tell us who
Is meant to pay? Oh God, oh God, what are we going
to do?
Boo hoo, boo hoo, goodbye EU – what are we going
to do?

We claimed a billion Turks were poised to flood across
our shore
Our country was at breaking point and couldn't take
one more

Tweedleboz and Tweedlegove

But without immigration then we'd all be in a stew
We need those guys – oh God, oh God, what are we
    going to do?
Boo hoo, boo hoo, goodbye EU – what are we going to
    do?

The whole of our economy is built on foreign backs
Their doctors and their workers bring us skills the
    UK lacks
All native Brits who want to be a cleaner, form a queue
Oh, no one, then? Oh God, oh God, what are we
    going to do?
Boo hoo, boo hoo, goodbye EU – what are we going to
    do?

'We want our sovereignty!' we cried, with oh such
    pious faces
And all the while we palled around with lunatics and
    racists
How good will independence feel when we're all broke
    and blue?
The world's gone mad – oh God, oh God, what are we
    going to do?
Boo hoo, boo hoo, goodbye EU – what are we going to
    do?

We're just a pair of toffs who thought this might help
our career
We only meant to blow the bloody doors off, now
we're here
We made a hundred promises, but none of them were
true
And so we're out – oh God, oh God, what are we
going to do?
Boo hoo, boo hoo, goodbye EU – what are we going to
do?

At the song's climax, Tweedleboz emitted a yelp and leapt into Tweedlegove's arms. The two immediately fell to the floor, where they rested a while.

'Ah well,' said Tweedleboz, picking himself up. 'At least now I get to be Prime Minister.'

He strode up to the podium and addressed the crowd:

'My fellow countrymen, it is with a profound sense of duty – and not a little reluctance – that I, Alexander Tweedleboz de Pfeffel Johnson, put myself forward to be your leader. For you see—'

Just then, he fell down dead, for Tweedlegove had knifed him in the back.

Tweedleboz and Tweedlegove

Sheepishly cleaning his blade, Tweedlegove kicked his brother's body to one side and took to the podium.

'As hard as that was,' he said, 'a sense of duty compelled me. For though I loved Tweedleboz, I knew in my heart of hearts that he could not have been our Prime Minister. I, on the other hand, should be. Does that sound good to everyone?'

'Obviously not,' cried the crowd in unison, 'on the basis that you're a creepy, duck-faced weirdo.'

'I see,' replied Tweedlegove, awkwardly fiddling with his glasses. 'In that case, I shall go off into the woods to sit on a log and think about what I've done.'

As the crowd dispersed, Alice happened to notice the Cheshire Cat sitting on an overturned apple-cart.

'Congratulations on your victory,' said Alice. 'You must feel like the cat who got the cream.'

'Oh yes,' said the Cat. 'This is a victory for real people, a victory for ordinary people, a victory for decent people.'

Alice frowned. 'Does that mean all the millions who voted the other way aren't decent and real?'

'That,' said the Cat, 'is for others to decide. I merely insinuate things.'

'Still,' said Alice, 'well done for winning. I should imagine you're excited to roll up your sleeves and get on with Brexit.'

'No,' said the Cat, 'I'm afraid I must announce my retirement. As far as I'm concerned, it's the people who *don't* want this who should have to sort it out.'

'But Puss,' said Alice, 'you promised Brexit would make the country so much better. Don't you want to be there when all your promises come true?'

Alas, the Cat had already started to vanish, beginning with the end of the tail and ending with the grin, which remained some time after the rest of him had gone. Soon the only clue that he had ever been there was the unmistakable smell of beer and Scotch-egg farts.

Chapter VIII

The Queen of Heartlessness

Alice felt that a walk might help her absorb what had just happened, and so she began to wander through the outskirts of the town. As she wandered, she noticed a great many people who were poor and hungry, and saw in their austere faces not a trace of hope. 'What are your views on Brexit?' she asked them, but each shrugged their shoulders and went on his or her way.

Eventually, Alice came upon a garden of red roses. There she saw a group of men shaped like playing cards, who were frantically painting the roses blue.

'I say,' said Alice, 'why are you engaged in this peculiar task?'

'These flowers are the wrong colour,' said the Five of Spades, 'and we must fix them before the Queen arrives.'

'She was only recently crowned,' the Three of Hearts added, 'and so everything must be perfect for her procession.'

'A new queen?' said Alice, 'How exciting! I suppose she must be very beloved of the people.'

'Nope,' said the Nine of Diamonds, 'no one really wanted her, but she came along all the same.'

At that moment, the Six of Clubs, who had been anxiously looking across the garden, called out, 'The Queen! The Queen!' and the four cards instantly threw themselves flat upon their faces. There was a sound of many footsteps, and Alice looked around, eager to see the monarch in person. Soon enough, she beheld a grand procession of playing cards: ministers and advisers and guardsmen. At the back of the pack, Alice noticed a group of Diamonds, who held aloft a magnificent golden throne. Sitting on this throne, resplendent in her crown, leather skirt and leopard-print heels, was the Queen of Heartlessness. Alongside her danced a minstrel, who strummed a lute and sang a song.

Theresa May, she made some hay
Reminding us of Thatcher
But now it's clear the Tories fear
Theresa may not match her

However, the minstrel was clearly not part of the official procession, for he was soon taken to one side and beaten by a pair of Clubs. As her throne passed by Alice, the Queen raised her hand, causing the whole train to stop abruptly. She turned, fixing Alice with an imperious glare, then demanded, 'What is your name, child?'

'My name is Alice, so please Your Majesty,' said Alice very politely, but she added, to herself, 'Why, they're only a pack of cards, after all. I needn't be afraid of them!'

'And do you know who *I* am?' said the Queen.

'You are Your Majesty, Your Majesty,' said Alice.

'Indeed,' said the Queen, 'and my reign will be much celebrated, for I shall deliver a Brexit that works for everyone.'

'Oh, that *is* a relief,' said Alice. 'And how do you plan to do so?'

The Queen's face reddened somewhat, but her voice remained steady.

'We shall strike a new trade deal with the EU that puts our country first,' she said.

'I see,' said Alice, not really seeing. 'But why would they agree to that? Surely they have every reason to make an example of us?'

The Queen, who would brook no contradiction, responded by screaming, 'Off with her head! Off with her head!'

Alice was rather taken aback, and not a little frightened. Fortunately, one of the advisers came up to whisper in the Queen's ear. He eventually managed to persuade her that, while she *could* have a child executed in the street, the optics would not be ideal. Now somewhat calmer, the Queen got down from her throne and walked over to Alice.

'Perhaps we got off on the wrong foot,' said the Queen. 'Let's shuffle the pack and start again, shall we? This garden is quite charming. Would you care for a game of croquet?'

'Usually I'd be delighted,' said Alice, 'but, on my way here, I saw a great number of people who were hungry. Shouldn't you be off helping them, rather than playing silly games?'

'Nonsense!' said the Queen. 'Once they become too hungry to move, they shall have the incentive to work harder. Now, take your mallet.'

Alice was handed a flamingo, and a hedgehog was set down for her to strike. She did so very reluctantly, and with great concern for both animals' feelings. A couple of rounds into their game, Alice turned to the Queen.

'Your procession is ever so grand,' she said. 'Where is it going?'

'I am off to Westminster,' the Queen replied, 'to trigger Article 50.'

'My,' said Alice, 'that sounds terribly important. I trust you've already triggered Articles 1 to 49?'

'Article 50,' said the Queen, 'is the means by which we shall leave the EU.'

'You must be very proud that your side won,' said Alice.

'Oh no,' said the Queen, whacking her hedgehog through a hoop. 'I campaigned for Remain. Well, if you can call what I did campaigning. I mostly just kept my head down.'

Horrified, Alice set her flamingo to one side.

'So,' she demanded, 'you thought Brexit was a wretched idea, but you're still determined to see it through?!'

'Naturally,' said the Queen. 'That is what is called leadership.'

'That is what is called madness!' said Alice. 'A decision that barely anyone understood is being carried out by a bunch of people who don't think it should happen!'

The Queen whipped around, causing her flamingo to squawk in alarm.

'How dare you?' said the Queen. 'How dare you suggest that this wild leap in the dark could be anything but an unqualified success?'

'What I'm suggesting,' said Alice, 'is that we shouldn't fling ourselves off a cliff and hope for the best. Surely a real leader would —'

Here the Queen stuck an accusing finger in Alice's face.

'I find you guilty,' she said, 'of the most heinous crime imaginable: *talking Britain down!*'

The cards all gasped in horror, and the Seven of Spades fainted.

'Though we already know that you are guilty,' the Queen continued, 'there must be a trial to find you so. Guards, tie her up! We shall take her with us... to London!'

Alice gave a cry of outrage as the Ace and Ten of Clubs placed handcuffs on her wrists, then threw her in the back of a carriage. As the procession set off once more, she sat there fuming to herself. Alice felt she was becoming rather tired of Brexitland. The Queen's retinue had advanced only a few steps when it came to sudden halt. Alice poked her head out of the carriage window to see what was going on. There, in the middle of the road, stood three playing cards in judges' wigs, who were blocking the procession.

'We're sorry, Your Majesty,' said the first of the three judges, 'but we must stop you there. You cannot lawfully trigger Article 50 without the consent of Parliament.'

'How dare you?!' howled the Queen. 'What right have some judges to enforce the law? I am your Queen! Have you any idea what I had to do to get this job?'

'Sit there while the other idiots shot themselves in the foot?' said the second judge.

At this, the Queen turned a deep shade of crimson.

'Do you really think you three can stop me?' said the Queen. 'A judge who founded a European law group, one who charged the taxpayer millions for advice, and an ex-Olympic fencer who is openly gay?'

'I don't see what that has to do with anything,' said the third judge.

The Queen turned to her guards, quite incandescent with rage.

'They are defying the will of the British people!' she said. 'All one hundred per cent of them, or fifty-two per cent, or whatever it was! OFF WITH THEIR HEADS!'

The Clubs advanced on the judges with their swords drawn. The Olympian produced his foil and cried 'En garde!', but his parries and thrusts would only hold them back so long. Alice turned away and sighed, for she could not bear to watch. When the judges' cries had been silenced, the whole mad procession was able to continue.

Chapter IX

The House
of Cards

Alice was woken by the sound of Bow Bells, cockney rhyming slang and people complaining about rent. She knew right away that she was in London. Alice looked out of her carriage window and beheld the Palace of Westminster: pulsating heart of Brexitland. Once they had reached its entrance, Alice was escorted inside by her two Club guards.

'Just so you know,' said the Ace of Clubs, 'We happen to think what they're doing to you is rotten.'

'Then let me go!' cried Alice.

'Sorry,' said the Ten of Clubs, 'I can't afford to lose this job, I've got a pack of kids to feed.'

Soon they arrived at the House of Commons, where Alice was very nearly thrown backwards by the appalling din.

'EEEERRRRRRAAAAAYYYYYYAAAAHHHH!' said half of the MPs. 'BBBBBLLLLLLLLLEEEEEEEEEE-GGGGGGHHHHH!' replied the other.

'Order! Order!' cried the Speaker, hammering a gavel against his head.

The Clubs removed Alice's handcuffs and showed her to her seat. From what she could tell, the MPs were debating Article 50, but they all spoke at the same time, so no one could hear anyone else. Alice saw the Caterpillar, reading questions from the public to precisely no effect. Tweedleboz had some-how come back to life and sat on the front bench with an enormous Elastoplast covering his back. Tweedle-gove stood nearby, looking apologetic.

The Speaker rose and, with a tremendous cry of 'ORDER!', was able to suppress the din.

'This behaviour from some of our Honourable Friends,' he said, 'is quite extraordinary. You were elected to represent the British people, not behave like a bunch of hooligans.'

As Alice wondered whether these things were mutually exclusive, the Speaker gestured to the opposition benches and shouted, 'Bob Common, MP for Grimton North!'

A card in his sixties stood up. He had a flat cap, a whippet and traces of coal on his kindly face.

'Mr Speaker,' he said, 'like many MPs, ah find mesel' in a geet tough spot. Grimton verted to leave by ninety-two per cent. Now, ah want to listen to the voices of me constituents. But nowt that ah have seen leads us to believe that Brexit would make their lives any bettah. So, for that reason, ah call upon me fellow Labour MPs to vert against —'

Suddenly, the Caterpillar leapt to his feet; Alice had never seen him so animated.

'You shut your mouth!' he shrieked. 'I have imposed a three-line whip, which means if you defy me, you shall be whipped by three men in a line! Now, can we please behave like an opposition and agree to everything the government says?'

The old MP sat back down, looking sad and confused.

Next, the Speaker bellowed, 'The Right Honourable Sir Julian Bigg-Fopp, MP for Little Frothingham-on-the-Wold!'

A card stood up who looked as though he was born with an entire silver spoon factory in his mouth. He had floppy hair, a tweed three-piece suit and, for some reason, wore a monocle in each eye.

Alice in Brexitland

86

The House of Cards

'Mr Speaker,' he said, 'as the House knows, I have been ardently pro-Brexit throughout this debate. It was my belief that our country needed change. However, I should be remiss were I not to acknowledge that there are those who fear said change; decent folks whose minds have been warped by the naysayers and the Remoaners. I hope that I may set their minds at ease with the following – very clear – explanation of how Brexit will work.

'*A Brexit is a numptious thing*
Its hubbish boons are clear
No fandan's heart will fail to sing
Once glamsome Brexit's here!

'*We'll have so much more limberlick*
And plap-plap in our zeets
No longer shall we jome and jick
At nugglers on our streets

'*The British udd, with vixfull meb,*
His silm lit up with yee
And pockets full of gronts and pebs,
Will cry "Toh-moo! Toh-mee!"

'So raise a glass of sloopy wame
And stuff your face with murl
Let Brexit be your firstborn's name
(Brextina for a girl)

'And klet not if you think my words
Sound quiggly and be-mimed
Have faith in Britain, not the nerds
Who say we're gerking splimed

'Don't frumligate your poor brain so
There is no cause to flex it
The only thing you need to know
Is Brexit does mean Brexit'

With that, the card fell poshly to his seat, and the surrounding MPs let out a 'MEEEEEEEYYYYYYYYYY-EEEEEEEHHHHH!' that shattered glass and loosened bowels.

Alice gazed at them in horror. 'Are these fools really to decide our future?' she said. 'They spend most of their time mooing like cattle, and when they do talk, it's absolute nonsense!'

Just then, the Queen of Heartlessness silenced the room with a deafening 'OFF WITH THEIR HEADS!'

Drawing herself to her full, regal height, she approached the dispatch box.

'The General Public have spoken,' said the Queen, 'and they have spoken clearly. No matter what some fancy mathematicians might say, we all know that fifty-two per cent is basically the same as one hundred. The fact of the matter is, the people want Brexit and they want it hard. For that reason, I have commissioned the world's largest catapult, one big enough to hold the entire nation. I call this device "Article 50". When I trigger Article 50, Britain will be thrown into space and fly straight into the sun. Only then shall we be truly independent.'

A majority of MPs cheered and applauded, for they agreed that this was a tremendous idea. The ones who disagreed kept quiet, in case anyone accused them of being out of touch. As for Alice, she could no longer hold her tongue. She raced to the middle of the chamber and climbed up on the despatch box. All eyes were on her, but Alice felt no trepidation, for she knew what she needed to say.

'ARE YOU ALL MAD?' she cried, then rounded on the Caterpillar: 'You! You claimed to oppose Brexit, and now you're telling MPs to vote for it in its most destructive form!'

'Hmm, yes,' said the Caterpillar, 'I *am* pretty rubbish.'

'And you!' said Alice, turning to the Queen. 'How can you say the public made a clear decision? All they had to go on was a series of grotesque creatures telling them riddles and lies!'

The Queen would have made her usual response had Alice not immediately moved on to Tweedleboz.

'What is wrong with you?' said Alice. 'This is about people's lives, for God's sake! You can't just play games like you're in the Debating Society!'

'Jumbly wumbly!' said Tweedleboz (which wasn't even a phrase).

'And you can't just go making stuff up,' said Alice. 'I can think of – oh, I don't know – *three hundred and fifty million* reasons why not.'

Tweedlegove rose to his feet.

'You're right,' he said. 'I shall go off into the woods to sit on a log and think about what I've done.'

Once he was gone, Alice took a deep breath and began her closing statement. 'Look,' she said, 'politicians lie – I may be seven years old, but I'm well aware of that. They lie, and they're not always wicked for doing so. We live in an incredibly complex world and there can be good reasons to lie. The right lie, in the right circumstances, can save someone's feelings, or even their life. And so we swerve, we finesse, we give partial answers, whether we're the Prime Minister or a schoolgirl. That's just how the world works. But, ladies and gentlemen, there is a difference between massaging the truth and murdering it. When we abandon the idea that there are basic facts that unite us all, we lose the ability to connect with anyone.'

(Pausing a moment, Alice wondered if she had been changed once more, for her vocabulary seemed greatly enhanced).

'Perhaps you will say the truth does not matter,' she continued, 'that it's merely the relic of a bygone age, as defunct as phrenology or the penny farthing. However, in taking such a view, you condemn us all to chaos, for when we throw away the truth, we create a vacuum, a vacuum that is soon filled by the worst aspects of humanity: our fears; our superstitions; our darkest and most primal instincts. So, go ahead, vote for this mad legislation. Tell yourself you're "respecting the will of the people", or that it's not worth the pain of opposing, or that we'll be able to sign some cushy deal with President Egg. But as you vote, do so in the knowledge that you are walking

91

our country off a cliff, and revealing yourselves to be nothing but a pack of spineless frauds!'

The MPs had been listening quietly up till then, but this was a bridge too far. Alice had questioned their integrity, and the outrage was felt across party lines. Rising as one, they unleashed an ear-splitting cry of 'BWWWWWAAAAAAAAAAAHHHHHHHH!' In the face of this heckle, Alice became angrier and angrier, until once again she felt herself beginning to grow. She quickly shot up to the size of an elephant and MPs scattered in every direction to avoid her expanding feet. This time Alice was so furious that she not only filled the room, but kept on going, and her limbs tore through the building as though it were a doll's house.

Alice did not stop growing until she towered over London, some six thousand feet tall. Birds flew around her fingertips and clouds left dewdrops in her hair. Alice could now see the whole of Brexit-land spread below, and she thought of all the people down there who would have to endure their leaders' madness. It seemed a shame to Alice, for, while Brexitland had its flaws – all too many, in fact – she could not help but be fond of the place. At any rate, she did not feel it deserved to be hurled into the sun.

Far below, Alice could just about hear the Queen cry, 'FIRE THE CATAPULT!' and, with a great yell, she felt herself flung up, up, up into the sky…

Chapter X

It Was All a Dream

Alice awoke with a yell.

'Darling, what's the matter?' said her sister.

'The catapult!' said Alice. 'They've thrown us into the sun! So much for democracy...'

'Catapult?' said Alice's sister. 'Thrown into the sun? I fear you've been in the sun for too long!'

'I was at the Houses of Parliament,' said Alice, bleary-eyed, 'where am I now?'

'My dear Alice,' said her sister, 'you and I are where we've been for the past few hours, sat here on the riverbank. Why, what a long slumber you've had!'

Alice looked around. All was as it had been: pleasant, green and tranquil. An evening sun glowed through the trees and gilded the lazy river.

'So, there was no White Rabbit?' said Alice. 'No drunken Tea Party and no Tweedle brothers?

No socialist Caterpillar, no Heartless Queen, no hateful Egg?!

Her sister let out a tinkling laugh.

'No, you silly thing,' she said, 'none of those creatures were here.'

'And,' said Alice, 'we haven't voted to leave the EU?'

'Leave?' said her sister. 'Of course not! Look, the news came through while you were asleep.'

Alice's sister held up her Samsung, with its browser open on the BBC homepage. A huge headline declared 'NO TO BREXIT – REMAIN PREVAILS WITH 99%'.

'And thank goodness for that,' said Alice's sister, 'for the alternative would have been mental.'

'Oh!' said Alice. 'I can't tell you how pleased I am! I was starting to think the world had descended into chaos.'

'Not a bit of it,' said her sister, 'in fact, the leaders of every EU nation are currently on their way to America, to attend a peace and prosperity conference hosted by President Clinton – my, that woman is an inspiration. Also, you know all of your favourite celebrities?'

'Yes?' said Alice.

'Well, not one of them has died! Not Prince, not Alan Rickman and *certainly* not David Bowie.'

'Thank goodness,' said Alice, 'for had we lost the Thin White Duke, I should have been beside myself!'

The more Alice thought back on her adventures, the more relieved she was to have woken up. She saw now that she had been wrong to wish away facts and figures, for one should never make a decision solely with one's gut. That road led to Brexitland, and, while it was certainly an interesting place to visit, to live there permanently would be a nightmare. 'Deep down,' thought Alice, 'I should rather exist in a world that's a bit boring than one with no rules whatsoever.'

Just then, something occurred to Alice, and she turned back to her sister.

'May I read your book?' said Alice. 'The one about the EU? At first I thought it looked horribly dull, for it had no pictures or conversations, but now I realise I should like to understand the subject.'

'I'm not going to lie,' said Alice's sister, 'it is very dull. But of course you may read it! Now,' she said, rising to her feet, 'let's go and have some supper.'

Alice took her sister's hand and set off home, towards a child-life of political stability and happy summer days. However, as they walked away, she noticed a dark shape on the bough of a nearby tree. It was the Cheshire Cat, smiling down at her.

'You, me and political correctness,' he said, 'we've all gone mad.'

'How can this be?' cried Alice. 'Was I dreaming then or am I dreaming now? Am I in a sane world dreaming of madness, or a mad world dreaming of sanity?'

Which do *you* think it was?

A Post-truth Poem

Scrolling through my Twitter page
Seeking vivifying rage
How I struggle to engage

Turning on the BBC
Feels like taking LSD
Breaking news is breaking me

Impotently I despise
Hollow fools with hollow eyes
Bludgeoning the world with lies

Give my brain a stomach pump
Nowt to like and lots to lump
In the age of Donald Trump

Nonetheless we can resist:
Though the liars tweet and twist
Light still penetrates the mist

Alice in Brexitland

Not all illnesses have cures
But, in spite of orange boors,
Life's great symphony endures

And its melancholy theme
Notes of laughter shall redeem
Life is more than just a dream